Curious George®
The Movie

George Icons

 alligator

 elephant

 balloon

 hat

 banana

 pants

 butterfly

 shirt

 city

 taxi

clouds

tree

Curious
George

The Movie

Meet Curious George

A Picture Reader

Adaptation by Jodi Huelin
Based on the motion picture story by Ken Kaufman
Motion picture screenplay by Ken Kaufman and David Reynolds
Based on the books by Margret and H. A. Rey

Meet .
 was a good

little monkey

and always very curious.

 lived in the jungle.

was curious about the

animals in his world.

 played with a baby .

He played with a baby 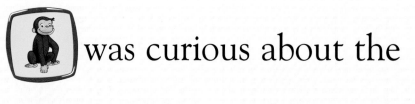.

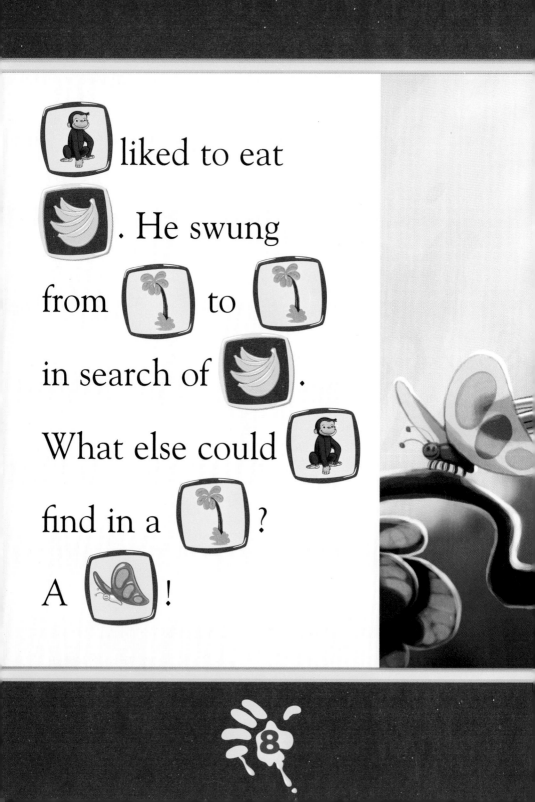 liked to eat . He swung

from to

in search of .

What else could

find in a ?

A !

One day, while sitting high in a 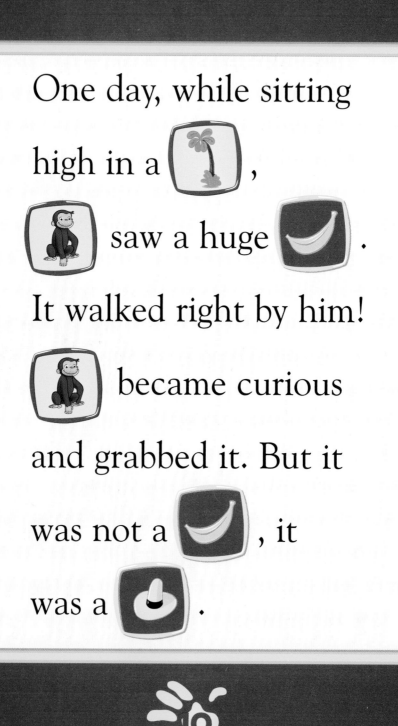, saw a huge . It walked right by him! became curious and grabbed it. But it was not a , it was a .

had found a man

dressed like a .

The man wore a

yellow .

He wore yellow .

And he wore a big

yellow  .

 liked the 🎩.
He wanted to try the 🎩 on, and so he did.
The man was surprised when 🐵 took his 🎩.
🐵 liked his new toy!

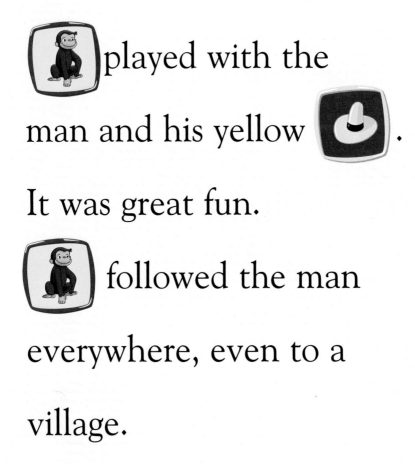 played with the man and his yellow . It was great fun. followed the man everywhere, even to a village.

16

Soon the man had to return home to the 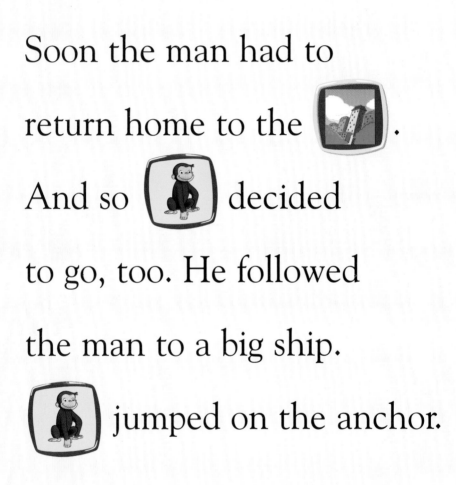.
And so decided to go, too. He followed the man to a big ship. jumped on the anchor.

Before he knew it,
 was in a .
Zoom! People rode
in fast  .
George rode a
 too.
Hold on, !

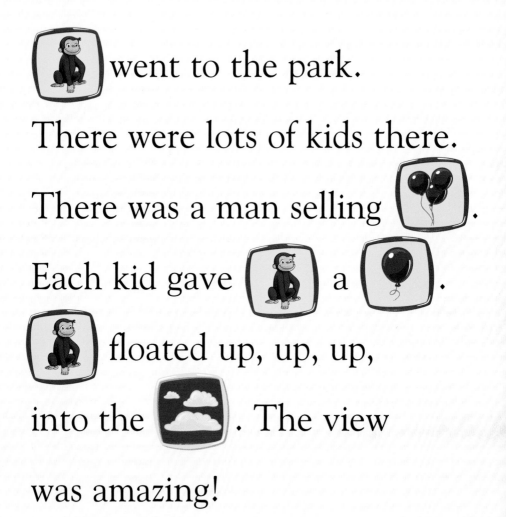 went to the park.

There were lots of kids there.

There was a man selling 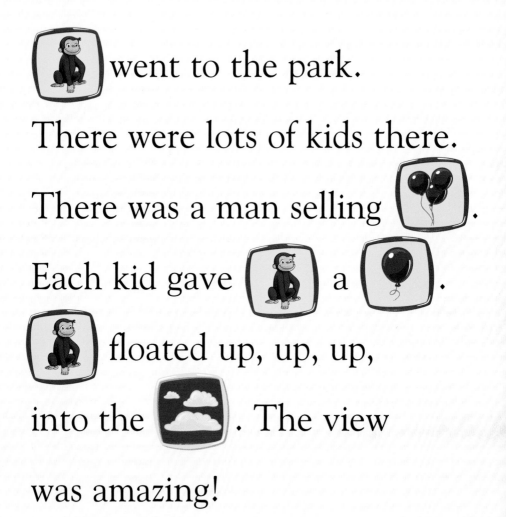.

Each kid gave a .

 floated up, up, up,

into the . The view

was amazing!

With , every day was an adventure!